Milton X

by

Matt Letourneau

To Brady
This is the
first signed
book!

Matt Letourneau

RoseDog❧Books
PITTSBURGH, PENNSYLVANIA 15238

RoseDog Books
585 Alpha Drive
Suite 103
Pittsburgh, PA 15238
Visit our website at *www.rosedogbookstore.com*

ISBN: 978-1-6495-7809-9
eISBN: 978-1-6495-7829-7

Dedicated to Mom, Dad, Nana, Papa, James Rice, and Cameron Robida
For Supporting Me

In Memory of:

Albert Joseph "Pepe" Letourneau, Jr.
(January 15, 1934 - April 09, 2001)

Jeanne Theresa "Meme" Picard Letourneau
(November 15, 1935 - June 20, 2002)

Peter Michael "Uncle Petey" Fitzgerald
(December 10, 1969 - April 21, 2011)

Paul A. "Twink" Glaude
(August 12, 1953 - August 16, 2013)

Yvette Marie "Aunt Yvette" Letourneau Roy
(May 09, 1939 - August 07, 2012)

Chapter I: The Origin Story

Georges Schwartz
1886

Wilson Johnson
1971

Milton Jay
Schwartz
1987

He was descended from superstars:

Georges William Wyatt Schwartz III (1836-1930) – his paternal fifth great-grandfather who saved a train of people from plummeting into a canyon in 1855 and founded the world-renowned Schwartz Car Company in 1921, before dying at the age of 93.

Wilson Thrill Johnson (b. 1900) – his maternal grandfather who, despite being handicapped from a 1933 bus accident, still managed to start playing baseball in 1961 and hit 893 home runs in his long career.

Milton Jay Schwartz (1965-2013) – his own father became an inspiring musician whose songs rose to become Number 1 on everyone's mind.

Now, you may be wondering who *he* is, right? Well, he is Milton. And this is his story.

Milton Jean Schwartz Jr. was a disappointment right from the start, when he was born on April Fool's Day, 2008. So, his parents named him Dropp Donnis Head and left him at an adoption center. After being adopted and renamed, Milton decided he had to be better than everybody thought he was. This is when his best idea yet popped up.

Milton knew that the only way to get some respect was to do something out of the ordinary. So, he recruited some friends. He went door-to-door in his neighborhood, knocking on the doors of his closest friends to create a group.

House #1 was his best friend, Charlie Lincoln. Charlie was a skinny little boy of about 10, who always had an '80s-style bowl-cut, a white

T-shirt, and blue overalls and lived in a small white farmhouse. After Charlie agreed, he was given the nickname "The Re-Enforcer."

From now on, he had to duct tape anything that he could in order to fix it.

"Thanks, Bud," he said to Milton after hearing the uplifting news. "The first thing I'll do is tape Pa's flipflop to that tree over yonder. It's the ultimate plan!" he said while rubbing his hands together evilly and laughing maniacally.

"Okay, on to the next house. Oh, if that's all right with you, Re-Enforcer," Milton said.

Milton and Charlie then hopped on their matching red 1955 bicycles and headed past a few eight houses to their friend Buddy Bricks'

house. Buddy was born on Christmas in 2009, making him between the ages of Milton and Charlie. He came from a family of nine brothers, so when the first two friends arrived, it wasn't all that quiet.

Milton knocked on the door and heard, "Buddy and Frankie! Get down here!"

A woman opened the door and shouted, "What do ya fellers want?"

"Can we—"

"No!" she said before slamming the large wooden door in Milton's face.

Buddy quickly reopened the door and asked why his two best friends were there.

"We were just wondering if you'd like to join our group of super-heroes!" Milton announced.

"Sure, hold on a second. Frankie! Get over here!" shouted Buddy.

Frank was Buddy's younger brother, who was only five years old and had basically no experience with anything.

"Milton and Charlie were just wondering if we'd wanna join their superhero game."

"Sounds great!" Frankie said.

"From now on, I shall be known as Lightning, Charlie is the Re-Enforcer, and now we need names for you two," Milton said.

He had to think for a moment, for he and Charlie already had "really" cool names and powers.

"Buddy, uh, you'll be—"

"I like books and reading," Buddy added.

"Very well, then. You can be Book Worm, Harnesser of the Books," Milton replied.

"What about me?" asked Frankie.

"You're, uhh, umm, hmm, The Sniffer," replied Milton once more.

"Let's go, I gotta leave this place," said Buddy.

And so, our heroes set out on the journey of a lifetime. They would rid the world of evil and save people in distress. But most of all, they were in for a lot of laughs and mess-ups.

Chapter II: Cameroon

On their bike ride to the next house, our comrades were greeted by a friendly visitor. As they rode down the street, they encountered a bright, colorful glow coming from an old house that was abandoned in 1934. It was a two-story house with large twisting vines running through every open window and door from top to bottom. The shutters creaked as of with pain, as the hinges slowly rusted and broke off. The four boys knocked on the gigantic, moldy door, but received no answer. They decided to do the only logical thing, which was to walk into this mysterious house and find the strange light.

As their shoes hit the marble floor, you could hear every step.

"I don't think this is such a great idea, pal," Charlie nervously said.

"Just hold on, I have a good feeling about this," said Milton bravely.

As they walked, the boys came upon a grand staircase crafted with beautiful wood and expensive gold, but unfortunately covered by vines and dust of the past 84 years. They climbed the many stairs to the next floor, which held a magnificent ballroom with a bright colorful light.

"Here it is!" Milton shouted with excitement, his voice rattling and echoing throughout the house.

The light was coming from nothing but a small box on the ground. After opening said box, Milton realized that it was a music box, and it began to play a peppy little song.

"Let's listen to it again!" said Frankie, filled with glee.

Milton restarted the music box with a small key he found lying near it, and the song began to play again. About halfway through, smoke began pouring out of the box. Soon enough, the whole ballroom was filled with a giant cloud of smoke.

"Who are you and why do you seek me?" boomed a deep voice.

"I'm Milton, and these are my friends: —Charlie, Buddy, and Buddy's brother Frankie." Milton told the cloud of smoke, at the same time noticing that Frankie was now sobbing loudly.

"Oh, you're kids, ain't you," said the cloud in a higher voice.

It then took on the form of a human with a long mustache complete with one curl on each end, long flowing hair, and an extended blue robe tied off with a golden ribbon.

"I am Cameroon, Guardian of Secrets and Holder of Promises," he told them. "Eleven years ago, Mademoiselle Frances Antoinette Cornelius bought this music box while on holiday. When she returned back here, it was her favorite thing. Then, Bob came," he began.

"Excuse me, who is Bob?" asked Milton.

"I'll get to that in one minute," replied Cameroon. "When Mademoiselle's parents, Jacques and Charlotte, returned from their vacation, they brought her a small brown puppy B, that she named Bob. She quickly became attached to the dog and was never able to realize that I was in her music box. When they moved out, I was left alone forever. Then you showed up and we can live together forever now!" Cameroon concluded.

"But, do you even know what year it is?" asked Charlie.

"Yeah, sure. It's 1934, right?" Cameroon nervously asked. After being told what the correct year was, 2018, Cameroon said, "In that case, I shall carry out my duty as Holder of Promises and grant each of you one wish. Frankie will go first."

"I wish for my own super-cool spowts cow," he said.

"What did he just say?" asked Cameroon.

"He wants a sports car," whispered Buddy.

"Very well, then."

Cameroon snapped his fingers. Soon enough, a bright red shiny sports car, modeled to fit Frankie's size, stood before them. Its vibrant colors gleamed, nearly blinding the crew, its mufflers roared, and its black leather interior glistened in the sun, which peered through the crooked window.

"Ooh! Me next!" shouted Charlie.

"I want a giant armor truck with nothing but black as its color and an unlimited supply of duct tape in the back, complete with speeds up to 200 miles per hour and a cow, just 'cause," Charlie burst.

"As you wish," said Cameroon, once again snapping his fingers.

The massive vehicle appeared before them, with thick black tires, a living room-sized back, and a cow living inside the back surrounded by a never-ending supply of duct tape.

"I know exactly what I want!" exclaimed Buddy.

"Yes?" Cameroon questioned. "And what would that be?" he asked.

"I want the exact same thing as Charlie, but instead of duct tape and a cow, I was wonderin' if I could have 500 books to replace the duct tape and a pig to replace the cow," Buddy exclaimed once again.

"Your wish is my command," Cameroon answered.

Sure enough, Charlie's truck reappeared, this time with a library and a pig, and a huge detailed painting of a pig on the side that read "Buddy Bricks" to distinguish it.

"I noticed that one member of your squad has not made his wish yet," Cameroon indeed noticed.

"Well, I guess, I'll give Buddy the power to summon and throw books with his mind," Milton quietly told Cameroon, as Buddy was looking at the ground, kicking a rat carcass.

"Done. And how 'bout yourself?" asked Cameroon.

"Umm...." Milton thought for a moment before having an amazing idea. "I know exactly what I'll have!" he shouted.

"I wish ...for a private island that has a magnificent mansion with five jet-speed sports cars, a private helicopter, a private yacht, and a beach. That way, we can have a hideout that we can all share!" Milton told Cameroon.

"That'll do!" said Cameroon, cracking his knuckles before eventually snapping the fingers of both hands, as this was a much larger wish. "And for my own wish," Cameroon continued, "I wish to be free," he stated.

Chapter III: The Search for #5

Now that Cameroon was free, he decided to bring Milton and his friends all the way to the Milton Cay, the new name for the private island. Upon arrival, Milton was crowned the first ruler, as his island was now a country. After choosing the flag, Milton and the others headed inside, where their steps once again echoed on the marble floor. Now, this wasn't just any mansion. Instead of being a mere three floors, this mansion (the Milton Manor) had 2,007 ten floors! Each friend got their own floor in the "house." Aside from the top and middle layers of the home was the garage, which was filled with high-tech sports cars and motorcycles. Each boy got their own car and bike, but there were five of each. Who was going to have the extra one of each?

Frankie proposed that they could use them as simply just "spares," but his idea was voted down.

"Let's take the helicopter back home, I'm positive we'll find somebody there," said Buddy.

So, the four of them took the elevator to the top floor. There, they were given a few flying lessons by Cameroon, who decided to stay and get the mansion set up a little bit more.

Milton, Charlie, Buddy, and Frankie all loaded up into the red private helicopter, started the engine, and began their 18-hour trek.

Upon arrival, they headed back to their neighborhood, and through the woods.

"Why do we always have to go in these creepy places, Milton?" asked Frankie.

Milton didn't answer, for he felt there would be something or someone there waiting for them. Sure enough, there was!

"Civilization!" cried a being.

"What was that?" asked Buddy.

"I don't—"

"Aahh!" roared the monster, beginning to chase the four boys. It gained speed, going faster and faster. This creature had ripped clothes, crooked yellow teeth, an oversized crooked nose, and long thick hair that looked as if it had been growing for 20 years.

After eventually getting tired out, Milton tried to talk to the creature. "Who are you and why must you chase us?" he yelled.

"I'm Bob Schwartz, and, I'm your cousin, Milton," Bob told them.

Milton didn't know what to say, he was speechless. A cousin? It was crazy. So, he said, "We are Milton, Charlie, Buddy, and Frankie, and we are starting a superhero group. Fortunately, we need a fifth one. Are ya willin' to join?" asked Milton bravely.

"'Course I am!" announced Bob.

"But first …you're gonna need some new clothes," replied Buddy.

Chapter IV: Back at Milton Cay

When our heroes returned to the island, they quickly noticed that Cameroon had unpacked all of their things and sorted it out in every room. After getting Bob some clothes, a shower, and a much-needed haircut, they let him get his things situated.

Frankie's room was every five-year-old's dream, for he had basically *too* much to do. He had an entire playground in his room that had a slide connecting down to his race-car bed, where he could sit and watch his television. To the side of this room was a huge desk with two computers, one for fun and games, the other for serious work such as researching.

Buddy's room had a King-sized bed, to make him love having no siblings even more, a television across from his bed, and the same computer setup as Frankie.

Charlie's room was basically his whole house inside of one room. It had Frankie and Buddy's computer and desk setup, but it also had a bed with carved animals in the side of it. The walls had paintings of cows, he had no TV, and instead a large sign that said his name in its place.

Milton's room, on the other hand, was completely obvious. He had a large library, twice the size of a regular public library, as well as the normal computer section. He had a television, again, and another separate library, where he would keep documents and journals of what was going on.

Bob's room was pretty much a farm, for all it had was hay for him to sleep on and a cow.

"This is amazing, Cameroon!" exclaimed Buddy, after seeing the new and improved home.

"Where's best bud, Milton?" asked Charlie.

"I don't—"

"Everybody, come to my room!" Milton yelled, beckoning the crew to follow him.

Milton pointed at his computer screen and shouted in excitement, "Look, our first job!"

Chapter V: Their First Mission

Milton, while browsing his computer, got a virus. When he checked it out, the virus directed him to a website called *Milton Cay News*. The headline was:

"Local nut goes crazy in the United States. Here's that story!"

The group of boys then proceeded to the video, which they watched.

"Hi, I'm Bill MacNamara and today a local man by the name of H.K. Villain broke out of jail and hasn't been caught. In 2000, a five-year-old H.K. stole a lollipop and was sentenced to life in prison. With the help of two friends, he successfully escaped. Fortunately for us, the other two jailbirds were caught. After reaching a local gas station, he dubbed himself 'The Villain' and—"

The computer screen started buzzing and a bright green line appeared across it.

"It is I. The Villain," said the line, moving in sync with a deep voice.

Just then, the lights flickered and then cut out.

"Cameroon!" shouted Charlie.

"Yes, I know. I'll stay here and try to fix the power. Meanwhile, you guys can go catch that evil man," answered Cameroon.

"I tracked down the voice of The Villain," replied Milton.

"All we need now is a name for our group," said Frankie.

"Boyz Klubb!" Bob blurted out.

"That'll do!" exclaimed Buddy.

Chapter VI: Catching the Villain

Now that Boyz Klubb had a location, all they needed to do was get to it.

So, they all crowded into the helicopter and took off. Upon arrival, they noticed that their GPS had led them to an elaborate mansion, a little bit smaller than Milton's.

"I don't think we have the right place," said Buddy.

"Well then, we'll just have to see for ourselves!" announced Charlie with pride.

The boys entered a gigantic room, crept up the marble stairs, and discovered a small glass door. On it, large black letters spelled out: J. W. Villain, CEO of Villain, Inc.

"Men, I think we've found our villain," Milton proclaimed.

One by one, the five boys entered the room, attempting to be as silent as possible.

"Welcome, children!" said a dark and menacing voice.

"H-hey there, s-stranger, I mean! M-mister!" said Charlie, shaking with fear.

"I am J. W. Villain, and I believe you know who I am," said the frightening man.

"Are you the guy that broke out of jail?" asked Frankie, like an oaf.

"What? No! That was my father, H. K. Villain," answered J.W.

"Oh. Well, where is he?"

"All I can tell you is that he's at the Villain Inc. Castle. That's it!"

"What's that?" asked Frankie.

"I said that's all I can tell you! Get out of my office!" the man boomed, standing right up in his suit and pointing at the door.

"Friends, I suppose all we can do now is head to Villain Inc. Castle," Milton said.

Chapter VII: The Villain's Evil Scheme

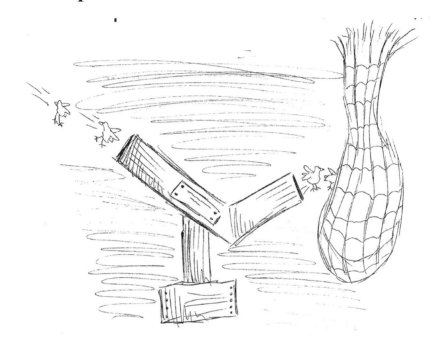

PEANUTS FIGHT I

Meanwhile, The Villain was busy thinking up ways of how to stir up trouble.

"I know, Gerald!" (Gerald was The Villain's assistant) "I'll steal all the chickens in the world and start a chicken army!" said The Villain. "But first, I must create a machine that can get them!" he laughed.

So, The Villain ran to his work station and gathered the tools he would need to create such a contraption. He grabbed his old toolbox and grabbed a bunch of metal, along with a welding machine, and created the most evil thing of all time:

"I'll call it: The Chickenator 8000!"

"Boss, you must gather the chickens! Your son told me that Boyz Klubb is on their way. And they have a five-year-old! A five-year-old!" Gerald yelled, flailing his arms.

"Okay," responded The Villain.

He flicked the switch into the "on" position, and the machine began to shake. After violently shaking for 10five minutes straight, The Villain shouted to Gerald to get a net ready.

After only 30ten more seconds, chickens starting blasting out the back of the Chickenator 8000, and into the net.

"The Peanut War begins!" The Villain told Gerald. "It begins!"

Chapter VIII: The Defeat of the Villain

Boyz Klubb landed at Villain Inc. Castle, not long after the chickens began flooding in.

Buddy had seen many movies before, and thought he knew what to do, so he hopped into a stranger's car upon arrival and drove into an elevator, climbed to the top of a 115-story building, and jumped right into The Villain's lair.

He smashed through the wall, swerved to the side, and jumped out of the car, before it exploded and blew the Chickenator 8000 to smithereens.

"Howard K. Villain, you're coming with us," said Buddy.

"Never!" yelled The Villain.

He grabbed a chair and attempted to fight off Boyz Klubb, but Charlie pushed him out the window and onto the roof of Villain Inc. Castle 2.0.

All five boys struggled to fight off Gerald and The Villain, but they eventually pushed him off the roof.

Luckily (but not for him), The Villain's button at the end of his lab coat got caught on the gutter.

"Help!" he yelled.

"I *might* change!" said the sly man.

Boyz Klubb all put their shoes above The Villain's fingers, before huddling together to whisper.

"Should we do it?" asked Frankie.

"I don't wanna hurt 'im," Charlie told them.

"Whatever, you took too long," said The Villain.

"Gerald!" he yelled.

Suddenly, from behind the boys came Gerald, complete with a large boot on his foot, ready to kick some little boys.

He cracked his knuckles and said, "Soon you'll be grub, Boyz Klubb," he laughed, picking up his foot.

Wham!

The boot came crashing down on the boys' behinds and knocked them off the roof of the 115-story building.

"Well, fellas, it looks like this is the end," sighed Charlie.

"Don't be so sure!" said Milton with glee.

"Huh?" asked his comrades.

"Look down!" Milton yelled.

What should await Boyz Klubb below, but a pile of chickens, all from the Chickenator 8000.

"Hurray!" shouted all five of the members.

"We're saved!"

When they landed on the chickens, the boys got up and heard somebody whisper, "Hey, Milton, over here!"

Can you guess who it was?

Why, it was Cameroon!

"The Queen received word about your heroism, and has invited you to her palace to be knighted!" Cameroon explained.

"All right!" shouted Frankie. "I'm gonna be a Prince!"

"Hahaha, not quite," Cameroon chuckled.

Chapter IX: Sir Milton

"Friends, we are gathered here today to celebrate the knighting of Milton, Charlie, Buddy, Frankie, and Bob. Boyz Klubb!" announced the Queen.

"Frankie, for your joy and bravery, I knight thee Sir Franklin Rudolph Bricks!" she said.

"Charlie, for your comedy and happiness, I knight thee Sir Charles Curly Lincoln!

"Bob, well, for being you, I knight thee Sir Bobbie Nothing Schwartz!"

"Buddy, for being kind and trustworthy, I knight thee Sir Donald J. Bricks!"

"Hey, Charlie, Buddy's name is Donald?" asked Frankie.

"How should I know, he's your brother," answered Charlie while clapping with the crowd.

"And now, Milton. For your strength, leadership, brain, and everything else that your friends have, I knight thee Sir Milton Jean Schwartz Jr.," said the Queen. "Your father would have been so proud of you," she whispered in his ear. "Congratulations!"

"Thank you," Milton whispered back, while shedding a tear and listening to the clapping of the crowd of people, all so proud of these five young men that had saved the world.

"Excuse me!" boomed another voice.

"Uh-oh," said Buddy.

"It's The Villain!" exclaimed Frankie.

"Yes, but he's also my brother," said the Queen.

To Be Continued?